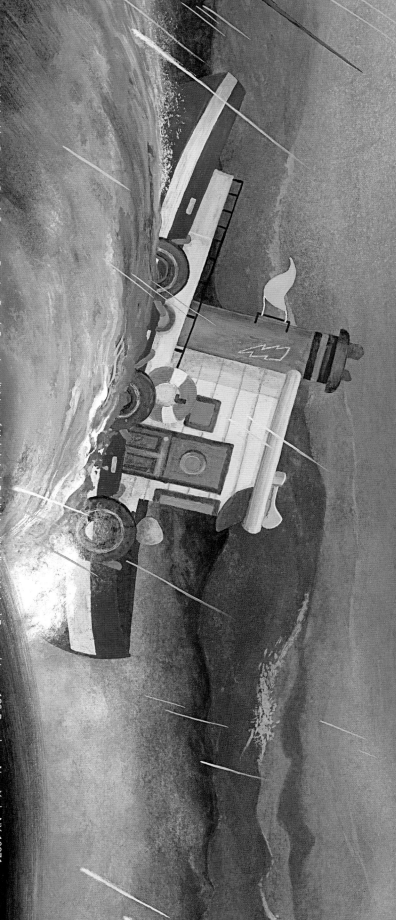

As a kid, RENÉ SPENCER developed a love for nature, art, travel, and foreign languages. She grew up speaking English at home and learned French in school before living and studying in Paris, France. When she is not busy working on picture books, you may find her watching movies from distant lands, reading, hiking, or taking care of bees.

RODOLFO MONTALVO is an illustrator and writer who grew up in Southern California speaking mostly Spanish at home and English at school. Today, whether on land, at sea, or in the air, Rodolfo is always working on a story, a drawing, a painting, or some kind of art project. He is the illustrator of the popular picture book *Dear Dragon*, written by Josh Funk. See more of his work at rodolfomontalvo.com.

René and Rodolfo live by the sea in the Los Angeles area and are always speaking in some combination of English, French, and Spanish. *Bye Land, Bye Sea* is their first picture book together.

Published by Roaring Brook Press • Roaring Brook Press is a division of Holtzbrinck Publishing Holdings Limited Partnership • 120 Broadway, New York, NY 10271 • mackids.com • Text copyright © 2024 by René Spencer and Rodolfo Montalvo. Illustrations copyright © 2024 by Rodolfo Montalvo. All rights reserved. • Our books may be purchased in bulk for promotional, educational, or business use. Please contact your local bookseller or the Macmillan Corporate and Premium Sales Department at (800) 221-7945 ext. 5442 or by email at MacmillanSpecialMarkets@macmillan.com. • Library of Congress Cataloging-in-Publication Data is available. • First edition, 2024 • Book design by Cindy De la Cruz and Mina Chung • The illustrations were created using watercolors, gouache, and graphite on watercolor paper. • Printed in China by RR Donnelley Asia Printing Solutions Ltd., Dongguan City, Guangdong Province • ISBN 978-1-250-24672-1 • 10 9 8 7 6 5 4 3 2 1

BYE LAND, BYE SEA

Written by **RENÉ SPENCER**
and **RODOLFO MONTALVO**

Illustrated by
RODOLFO MONTALVO

ROARING BROOK PRESS

New York

I'm lost.

Soy náufrago.

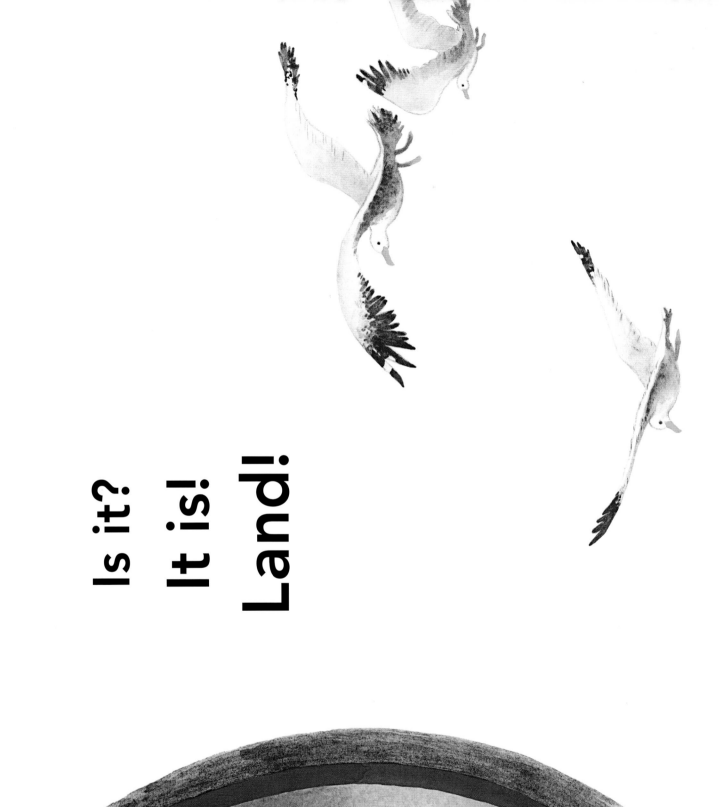

Is it?
It is!
Land!

Pero ¿es amigo o enemigo?

¡Sí, es un barco!

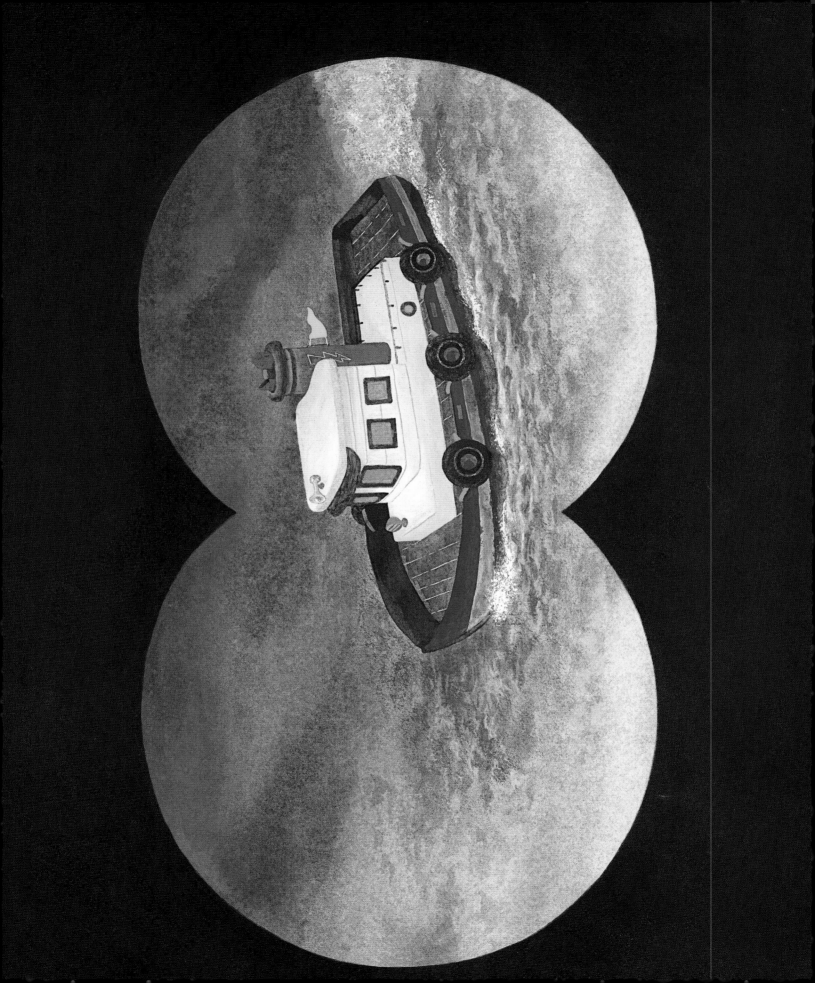

I think I see someone!

¡Hay una persona!

¿Será un barco
de rescate?

I need to secure
the boat.

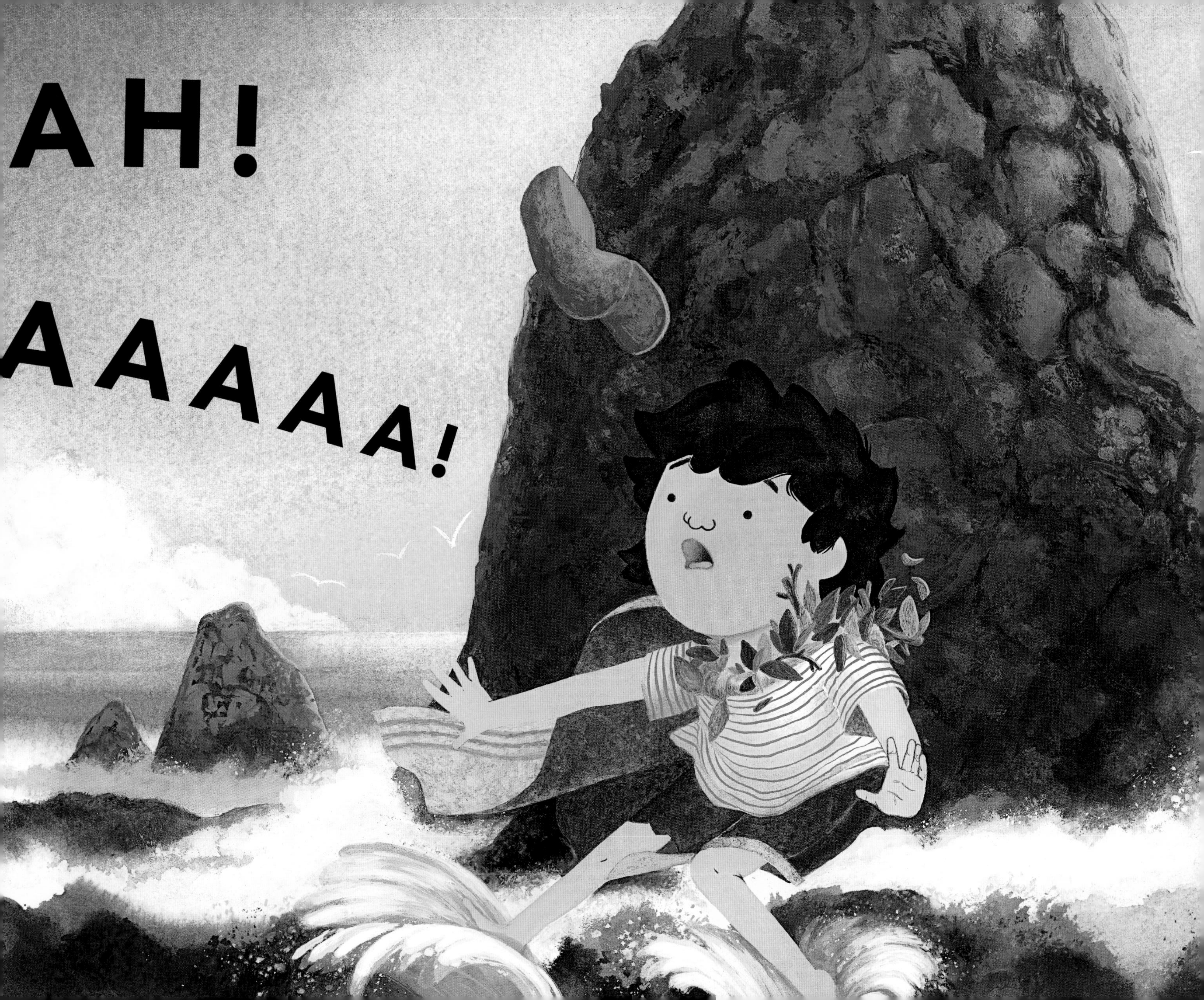
AH!
AAAAAA!

That was just a boy . . .

Era solo una niña . . . .

Hi.

Hola.

This is my boat.

I'm the captain.

Esta es mi tienda
de campaña.

Bienvenida.

Let's go!

Viene una tormenta.

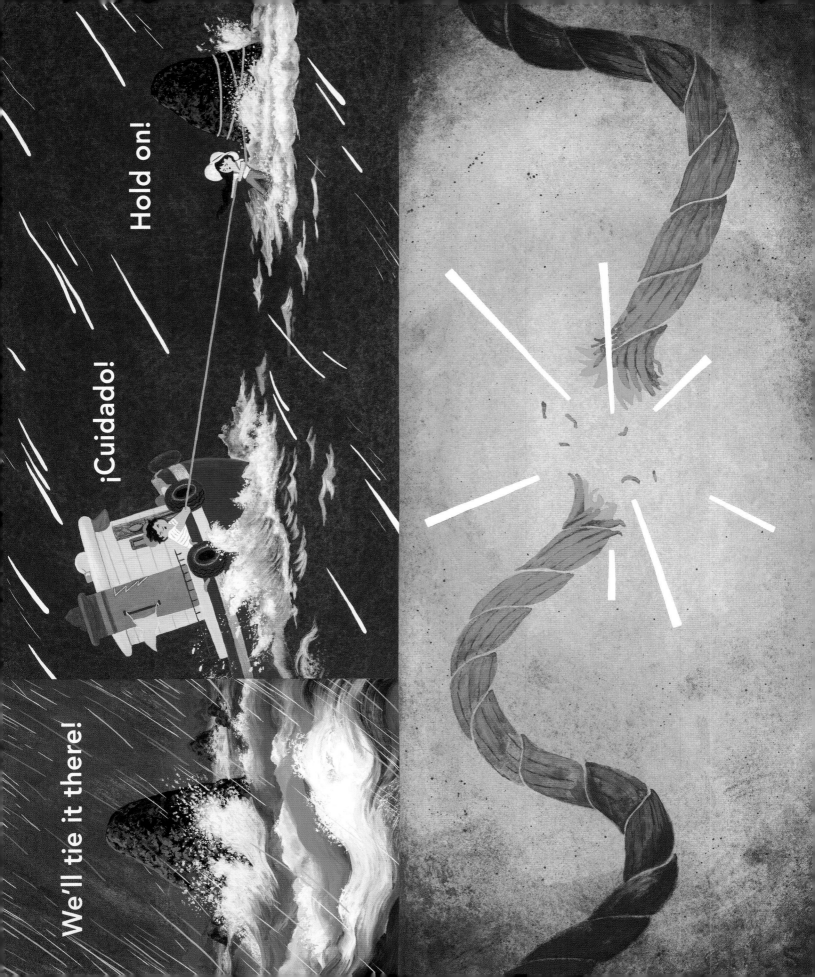

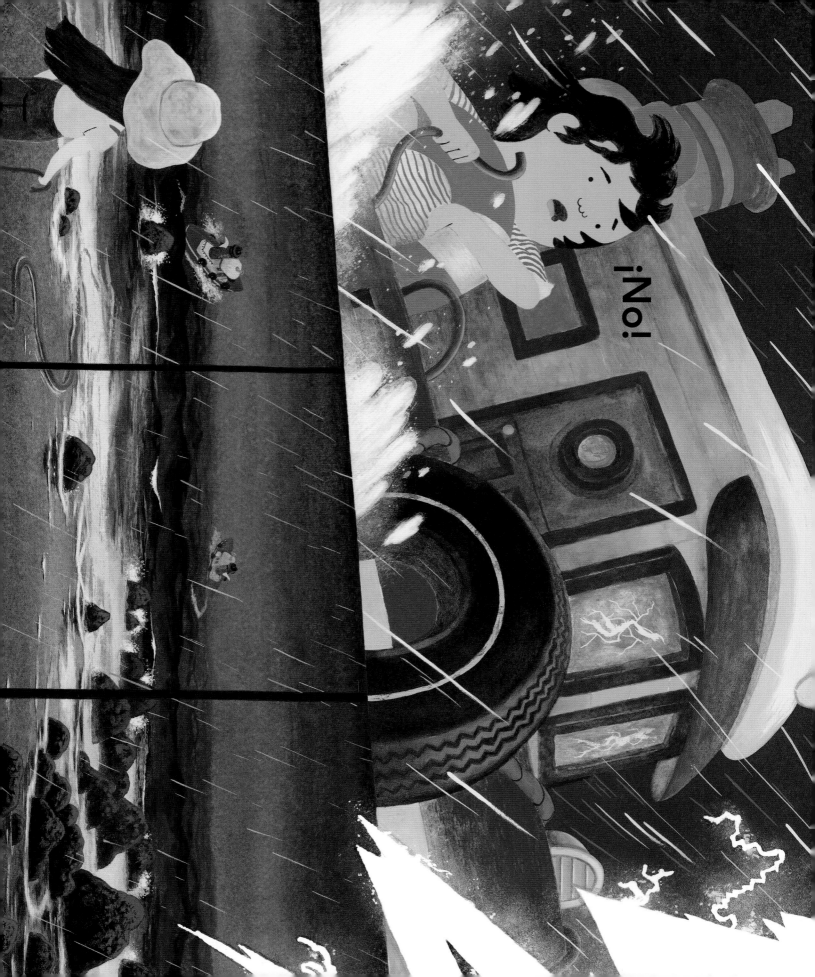

¿Dónde estás?

Where are you?

Look!